THIS CANDLEWICK BOOK BELONGS TO:

_____

_____

_____

_____

For Michael Philip
J. C.

———————————

For Amelia
S. L.

Text copyright © 1995 by June Crebbin
Illustrations copyright © 1995 by Stephen Lambert

First U.S. paperback edition 1996

The Library of Congress has cataloged the hardcover
edition as follows:

Crebbin, June.
The train ride / June Crebbin ; illustrated by
Stephen Lambert. — 1st U.S. ed.
Summary: A journey on a train provides excitement,
nice scenery, and pleasant anticipation.
ISBN 1-56402-546-2 (hardcover)
[1. Railroads — Fiction.] I. Lambert, Stephen,
1964 – ill. II. Title.
PZ7.C86Tr   1995
[E] — dc20   94-15156

ISBN 1-56402-842-9 (paperback)

10 9 8 7 6 5 4 3 2 1

Printed in Hong Kong

This book was typeset in Rockwell.
The pictures were done in chalk pastel.

Candlewick Press
2067 Massachusetts Avenue
Cambridge, Massachusetts 02140

CL 5/97

The Train Ride

June Crebbin

CANDLEWICK PRESS
CAMBRIDGE, MASSACHUSETTS

illustrated by

Stephen Lambert

We're off on a journey   Out of the town —

What shall I see?   What shall I see?

Sheep running off
And cows lying down,

That's what I see,
That's what I see.

Over the meadow,
Up on the hill,

What shall I see?
What shall I see?

A mare and her foal
Standing perfectly still,

That's what I see,
That's what I see.

There is a farm
Down a bumpety road —

What shall I see?
What shall I see?

A shiny red tractor
Pulling its load,

That's what I see,
That's what I see.

Here in my seat,
My lunch on my knee,

What shall I see?
What shall I see?

A ticket collector
Smiling at me,

That's what I see,
That's what I see.

Into the tunnel,
Scary and black,

What shall I see?
What shall I see?

My face in a mirror,
Staring back,

That's what I see,
That's what I see.

After the tunnel,
When we come out,

What shall I see?
What shall I see?

A gaggle of geese
Strutting about,

That's what I see,
That's what I see.

Over the treetops,
High in the sky,

What shall I see?
What shall I see?

A giant balloon
Sailing by,

That's what I see,
That's what I see.

Listen! The engine
Is slowing down —

What shall I see?
What shall I see?

A market square,
A seaside town,

That's what I see,
That's what I see.

There is the lighthouse, The sand, and the sea . . .

Here is the station —

Whom shall I see?

There is my grandma

Welcoming me . . .

Welcoming

me.

JUNE CREBBIN was a teacher until she retired to write full time. She was taking a class on a field trip to a railroad museum when she first thought of the idea for this book. "What I really wanted to do most was get the rhythm of the train," she says. June Crebbin is the author of *Fly by Night,* also illustrated by Stephen Lambert, *Danny's Duck,* illustrated by Clara Vulliamy, and *Into the Castle,* illustrated by John Bendall-Brunello.

STEPHEN LAMBERT says about *The Train Ride,* "I liked the sense of continuous motion and the idea of a big red train chugging through the fields." He is also the illustrator of June Crebbin's *Fly by Night,* and of *What Is the Sun?* by Reeve Lindbergh.